# Yossi's Goal

## Ellen Schwartz

ORCA BOOK PUBLISHERS

**Library and Archives Canada Cataloguing in Publication**

Schwartz, Ellen, 1949-
Yossi's goal / Ellen Schwartz.

(Orca young readers)
ISBN 1-55143-492-X

I. Title. II. Series.

PS8587.C578Y68 2006      jC813'.54    C2006-903145-2

First published in the United States, 2006

**Library of Congress Control Number:** 2006928084

**Summary:** Yossi, a Jewish immigrant boy in Montreal, longs to play hockey, but when his father becomes ill and cannot work, all Yossi's hard-earned savings must go to help the family, not to buy skates.

Free teachers' guide available: www.orcabook.com

Orca Book Publishers gratefully acknowledges the support for its publishing programs provided by the following agencies: the Government of Canada through the Book Publishing Industry Development Program and the Canada Council for the Arts, and the Province of British Columbia through the BC Arts Council and the Book Publishing Tax Credit.

Cover design by Doug McCaffry
Cover & interior illustrations by Silvana Bevilacqua

**In Canada:**
Orca Book Publishers
Box 5626 Stn.B
Victoria, BC  Canada
V8R 6S4

**In the United States:**
Orca Book Publishers
PO Box 468
Custer, WA  USA
98240-0468

www.orcabook.com
Printed and bound in Canada.
Printed on recycled paper.
09  08  07  06 • 6  5  4  3  2  1

In memory of Elaine Zuker and Irving Bregman

The author would like to thank Éléonore Lebeuf-Taylor
and Glen Taylor; Ruth and Bernie Rosenberg;
James and Lynn Hill; Amy, Merri and Bill Schwartz;
and the Jewish Public Library in Montreal.

# Chapter One

Yossi took the stairs two at a time, racing up the three flights to his family's apartment in a rundown building. Night was already falling, and he was supposed to be in before dark. He knew that Mama and Papa worried when he was late—after all, they lived in Montreal now, no longer in a small village where everyone looked out for everyone else. But he and his new friends, Abie, Benny, Louie and Milton, had been having so much fun playing hide and seek, he'd completely forgotten about the time. It was only when the gas lamps were lit that he had noticed the gathering darkness.

He burst in the door. "Mama, Papa, I'm sorry, I—"

He stopped short. Everyone was crowded together in the tiny kitchen, and there was a woman Yossi didn't recognize sitting at the table.

"Yossi," Mama said in a tense voice, "come and meet Mrs. Belnick. She's from the *landsmanschaft*."

Yossi's first feeling was relief—he wasn't going to get in trouble, at least not in front of company. But then he began to wonder why Mama sounded so strange. He had no idea what the *landsmanschaft* was, but plump Mrs. Belnick looked perfectly pleasant.

"Good afternoon, young man," she said with a smile.

"Good afternoon, ma'am."

Nothing wrong with her, Yossi thought. It was everybody else who looked odd, holding their tea cups stiffly, with grim expressions on their faces.

Yossi's family—Mama, Papa, Yossi and his seventeen-year-old sister, Miriam—

shared the small flat with the Bernsteins—Daniel, Miriam's soon-to-be-husband, and Sadie, his widowed mother. Because they owned only four chairs, the women sat around the small wooden table, while Papa and Daniel leaned against the wall. Squeezing between the two men, Yossi tried to figure out what was going on.

There was a furrow in Mama's forehead as she poured tea for Mrs. Belnick. Could it be the teacups? Yossi wondered. He knew that Mama was ashamed of the chipped cups. They were all the family had been able to afford when they had arrived in Canada six months earlier, in the spring of 1891. They had fled Braslav, their Russian village, after Russian soldiers had started attacking Jewish settlements. They hadn't been able to take more than a few clothes and their prayer books with them. Now, every time someone came to visit, Mama fretted about serving tea in the secondhand cups.

But it couldn't just be the teacups, because *everybody* looked tense.

*What was the matter?*

Meanwhile, if Mrs. Belnick noticed the tension, she ignored it, chatting away as if nothing was the matter. "Now, the best place to buy eggs, as I'm sure you know, is Litvak the greengrocer..."

Like the rest of them, she spoke Yiddish, the language that the Jewish immigrants from Eastern Europe spoke among themselves. Yiddish at home, at work, in the market. Hebrew in schul and, for the children, at lessons. Scraps of Russian or Polish, Romanian or Czech, plus the odd new word of English and French, which the children picked up in the neighborhood and taught their parents.

Finally, Mrs. Belnick put down her cup. "Now," she said, "the season is turning, and it'll soon be freezing cold. Montreal winters—*oy*, the snow, the ice, the bitter wind! So I've brought a few things from the landsmanschaft to help you through your first winter."

She opened a large cloth bag at her feet and suddenly Yossi understood.

She was there to give them charity because they were too poor to buy warm things for themselves. That was why Mama had the furrow in her forehead. That was why Miriam and Sadie had the grim expressions. That was why Papa and Daniel were standing so stiffly.

"We've never accepted charity from anyone," Papa said. His face was like stone.

"It's not charity, Mr. Mendelsohn," Mrs. Belnick said, "it's *tzedakeh.*"

"What's the difference?" Daniel growled.

Mrs. Belnick wagged her finger, though she continued to smile. "A big difference. It's not a handout; it's simple justice. Those with more helping out those with less. There's no shame in it."

"Except when you're on the receiving end," Daniel muttered.

"So," Mrs. Belnick went on, "when you get on your feet, it'll be your turn to help. That's what the *landsmanschaft* is for— to help fellow immigrants get settled."

Daniel grunted. Mrs. Belnick ignored him and reached into the bag. "Now, for you, Mrs. Mendelsohn, a nice warm head-scarf." She pulled out a blue *babushka* and handed it to Mama.

Mama took it without looking at it and laid it in her lap. "Thank you," she whispered. The expression on her face was so pained that Yossi looked away.

"And I also have one for you, Mrs. Bernstein," Mrs. Belnick said, giving a brown *babushka* to Sadie. Yossi noticed that one edge was frayed. Sadie murmured her thanks in a low voice.

"Now, for you, young Miriam, something to keep you toasty on those cold winter nights." Mrs. Belnick handed Yossi's sister a faded red flannel nightgown.

Part of the rick-rack trim was torn and hung loosely from the bodice. Yossi saw Miriam, then Mama, glance at the rip. Mrs. Belnick's eyes followed theirs. "A small tear," she said apologetically.

"Miriam's clever with her needle," Mama said tightly. "Aren't you, Miriam?"

Miriam nodded, her hands bunching the nightgown into a small ball.

"Now, what's next?" Mrs. Belnick said, reaching deeper into the bag. "Oh, yes. For you, Mr. Mendelsohn." She handed Papa a gray wool winter hat. It had earflaps and was lined with flannel. The chin strap was broken.

Papa's face colored. "I don't want it."

"But Mr. Mendelsohn, just look at it, it's so warm," Mrs. Belnick said, sounding distressed. "You need a warm hat to get you through the winter."

Papa opened his mouth to speak but coughed instead. It was a loose rumbly cough. Listening to the familiar sound, Yossi realized that Papa had been coughing for several weeks now. Before Papa could reply, Mama said in a low voice, "Just take it, Avram." Papa clutched the cap, his mouth set in a line.

"Now it's your turn, young man," Mrs. Belnick said, nodding at Yossi. His heart beat fast. He hated the idea of taking hand-me-downs, but still, he couldn't help wondering what she had for him.

His breath stopped when he saw it. A

winter coat. Navy blue, hooded, with two deep pockets and wooden toggles that fastened up the front. One of the pockets was torn, and there were several tiny burn holes spattered over the coat. But it was splendid. It was the most wonderful thing he had ever owned.

"Oh, Yossi!" Mama gasped, and Yossi could see that even she was dazzled. "Put it on."

It fit perfectly. Yossi fastened all the toggles and put the hood on and off and on again. He thrust his hands into the pockets and hugged the coat to himself.

"Imagine casting off such a coat," Mama said incredulously.

Mrs. Belnick shrugged. "Perhaps the child outgrew it. You know how boys grow." She smiled, and Yossi sensed that she was relieved that finally someone was happy to accept one of the donations. *Happy!* He never wanted to take the coat off, not even to let Mama sew the torn pocket.

"Now, finally, for you," Mrs. Belnick said, nodding at Daniel, "a nice warm sweater."

She pulled a thick gold and green woolen sweater out of the bag. "There's a hole in the elbow," she went on, poking her finger in, "but nothing that a little darning won't fix—"

"I don't want it," Daniel said.

"I'm sure your mama can mend it for you—"

"I won't take it." Daniel folded his arms.

"Now, Daniel—" Sadie began.

"No!" Daniel snapped. "No, Mama," he went on in a lower voice, "you can call it charity or *tzedakeh* or whatever you like, but I'm not taking it. You know where these things come from? From our bosses, the factory owners, and their wives and children. Let them pay us a decent wage instead, and I'll buy my own sweater. Until then, I'm not wearing their castoffs!"

Sadie looked mortified. "Please, Daniel, don't make a fuss."

"I'm sorry, Mama, and no offense to you, Mrs. Belnick. But I won't take the sweater. I'd rather freeze!"

Suddenly Yossi felt uneasy. Now that

Daniel put it that way, he didn't like taking handouts either. Should he give back the coat?

The trouble was, he needed it. They all needed the hand-me-downs.

None of them had expected to find things so hard in Canada. All the way across Europe, as Yossi and his family and fellow villagers ran from town to town, hiding in forests and barns and cellars, fleeing the soldiers and angry mobs, they had held the image of Canada in front of them. All during the months-long sea voyage, they'd dreamed about the better lives they'd have. Canada—a beautiful place of forests and rivers. Canada—the land of opportunity, where a family could work hard and prosper. Canada—a free country, where you didn't have to be afraid because of your religion or your beliefs.

Some land of opportunity!

Free, yes. There were no soldiers dragging Jews out of their beds and beating them or worse. You could worship as you pleased, say what you thought, even print your opinion in the newspaper.

But what good was freedom, Yossi wondered, if you were only free to be poorer than before? From the time that he and the others were disgorged from their steamship on the banks of the Saint Lawrence River, they'd found themselves huddled in a squalid neighborhood at the foot of The Main, the busy boulevard that ran north from the river's docks. There, thousands of Jewish refugees from Eastern Europe lived in broken-down tenements. Rents were so high that people were forced to live two, sometimes three, families to a household. That was why there were two families squeezed into Yossi's third-floor flat. The four Mendelsohns slept in one bedroom. The Bernsteins—mother and son—occupied another. All of them shared the tiny room that served as kitchen, dining room and parlor. Along with dozens of neighbors, they used an outdoor privy and pumped cold water from a hand pump on the street.

Papa and Daniel worked in a garment factory—sweatshops, they were called—alongside hundreds of other men, hunched over electric sewing machines for twelve hours a day. Miriam and Mama and Sadie did the same thing at home, taking turns at a rented machine and doing handwork on the side. Yossi and his friends helped their families out by lugging bundles of cut-out garment pieces to homes to be sewn and then lugging the finished garments back again. All for a couple of dollars a week for a family. Barely enough to live on, never enough to save, to move to a bigger flat, to buy warm clothes.

Which was why they had to take handouts. *Tzedakeh*, Mrs. Bernstein called it. Castoffs, Daniel said.

*I'd rather freeze.* Yossi tried out the phrase in his mind. He pictured himself thrusting the coat back at Mrs. Belnick and declaring in noble tones, "No charity for me. I'd rather freeze!"

But then he hugged the coat to himself.

He'd never owned such a thing. He pictured the old tattered coat he'd brought with him from Braslav, with its too-short sleeves and thin lining and frayed cuffs. He imagined how warm and cozy he'd be in his new coat this winter, how dazzled his friends would be by the smart hood and the clever toggles.

Would it do any good if he refused the coat? Would it help anything if he froze? If he got sick, like Papa, and couldn't do his job and contribute the few pennies he made to the family?

Of course not.

Feeling only slightly uneasy, Yossi snuggled deeper into the thick warm wool of his beautiful new coat.

# Chapter Two

"Today," Papa announced one Saturday morning soon after Mrs. Belnick's visit, "since our Rebbe is sick, why not go to a proper *schul* for Shabbas services? We'll go to Congregation Sha'ar Hashonayim."

Yossi gaped. He'd never been there, but he knew that Congregation Sha'ar Hashonayim was one of Montreal's oldest—and grandest—synagogues.

"Are you crazy, Avram?" Mama said. "We don't belong there. It's for Uptowners."

"So? We're all Jews, aren't we?" Papa said.

"Right," Daniel said with a grin. "Those rich snobs can't keep us out."

Ever since they'd arrived in Canada, the Mendelsohns and the Bernsteins had been gathering with other Braslav families on Saturday mornings in the tiny flat of their old Rebbe. The Rebbe didn't have a *schul* or a congregation of his own here in Canada, but he was still a Rebbe, and it gave the Braslav folks comfort to have him lead them in Sabbath prayers. Yossi had never imagined going anywhere else—least of all to the uptown schul. But the Rebbe had a cold, and they needed to go somewhere.

Mama argued that they'd be out of place, but Papa insisted. So off they went, Yossi proudly wearing his new winter coat, for it was early December and a light dusting of snow had fallen the night before.

As they walked north up The Main, Yossi noticed that the houses grew ever grander, changing from the broken-down tenements of the immigrant district to nicer-looking apartment buildings with painted window frames, then to modest brick homes and finally to mansions with wrought-iron gates surrounding sculpted bushes and vast lawns. He was just about to ask Papa who lived in such fancy homes, when one of the gates opened. A family came out, a father, a mother and two children, and started walking in the same direction as Yossi's family. All were richly dressed. All were carrying Hebrew prayer books.

Jews! Jews lived in that house!

Yossi turned to Papa. "Papa—can it be?" he whispered.

Papa nodded. "Jewish factory owners and merchants," he said in a low voice. "They came over long ago, established themselves, started businesses. They learned English, learned the English ways. That was how they were able to fit in with the wealthy people, the leaders. So they prospered."

Daniel, who had been walking ahead with Miriam, turned around. "Steiner lives up here," he said bitterly. "One of these palaces must be his."

17

"Imagine!" Mama said, shaking her head.

When they arrived at the synagogue, Yossi shuffled with Papa and Daniel into one of the wooden pews on the main floor, while Mama and Miriam and Sadie went up to the balcony, where the women prayed. Yossi looked around—and immediately felt overwhelmed. Row after row of velvet-covered pews filled the enormous sanctuary, and the ceiling soared high overhead. Scarlet and gold tapestries depicting the Star of David decorated the *bima*, the raised platform at the front. The ark containing the Torah, or holy scrolls, even had jewels on it!

Yossi had never seen a *schul* like it. Back home in Braslav, the *schul* had been a hut with simple wooden benches, and the Torah had been kept in a plain pine cupboard. What did Yossi know from jewels and velvet?

As Yossi, Papa and Daniel seated themselves, the elegant man next to Yossi took one look at his shabby trousers and worn boots and moved slightly away. The look on his face seemed to say, What are *you* doing here?

*Mama's right,* Yossi thought with dismay. *This place isn't for the likes of us.*

But then the Rebbe and cantor began to sing the Sabbath prayers, and the melodies swept Yossi up in their familiar comfort. The prayers were the same as those they'd chanted in Braslav. And the Torah—even though this one was encased in a blanket of blue silk and crowned with a golden cap, instead of wrapped in a simple cotton quilt—was still the Torah. He and his family were Jews, after all, and Sabbath was Sabbath, whether in a hut or a palace. God didn't care if they were richly dressed or clad in rags.

The service progressed as usual, and soon Yossi was joining Papa in singing the final hymn.

"*Shabbat shalom,*" the Rebbe intoned from the *bima*, and all around Yossi men shook hands and patted each other on the shoulder.

"Good Sabbath...good *Yuntov*..."

As Yossi, Papa and Daniel made their way toward the front door to wait for the women outside, along came a short man with an imposing belly, florid cheeks and a balding head. His stylish black coat hung open, revealing a shiny black waistcoat over a gleaming white shirt. A golden watch chain dangled from a pocket of the waistcoat. "*Shabbat shalom*," he bellowed to all he passed and was greeted in return.

Yossi knew who he was—Saul Steiner, the owner of the garment factory where Papa and Daniel worked and where Yossi picked up and dropped off the bundles. Saul Steiner, who lived in one of the mansions they'd passed that morning. Yossi had seen him at a distance, across the sweatshop floor, but never up close. He doubted whether Mr. Steiner knew who he was—or who Papa or Daniel were either, for that matter.

As Mr. Steiner approached them, Papa lowered his eyes, touched his hand to his woolen cap and said, "*Shabbat shalom*, sir."

Mr. Steiner gave no reply. He simply looked past them as if they weren't there and moved on, greeting someone else.

Yossi's ears burned. "Papa, he snubbed you—," he began.

Papa grabbed his arm. "Yossi, *shaaah!*"

"But Papa—"

"Not here!"

Yossi looked at Papa. His father's cheeks were red. So why hadn't he said anything? Why had he let Mr. Steiner treat him like that?

Papa never used to humble himself like this, Yossi thought. Not even back in Russia, not even to the Cossacks had Papa bowed his head.

And now, to see Papa lower himself before a man like Mr. Steiner!

They found the women and set off down the synagogue's broad steps. Yossi preened a little, wondering if anyone would notice his finery.

No one did.

Just as they reached the end of the

front walk, a group of boys ran toward them. The leader, Yossi saw, was a little older than he, a stocky boy with curly, dark brown hair and pink cheeks. He had on a smart black winter coat with brass buttons and soft leather boots that buckled above the ankles.

Leading the others, he circled close to Yossi. "You enjoying your new coat?" he said, his eyes dancing. The other boys giggled.

Yossi nodded. "Yes, I am! It's—"

The boy grabbed one of the toggles and leaned into Yossi's face. "Good, 'cause it's my *old* coat, and I don't want it anymore. My old *shmata*! I threw it away!"

He let go of the toggle and darted away, followed by his guffawing friends.

Yossi felt his ears grow warm. He started after the boy. "Why, you—"

Papa jerked him back. "Yossi, no!"

Yossi struggled to free himself, but Papa held him fast. "But Papa—"

Papa turned Yossi to face him. "Yossi, you know who that is?"

"No, and I don't care!" He broke away. Again Papa pulled him back.

"It's Max Steiner. Steiner's boy."

"I don't care who he is. He can't get away with that—"

"Yossi, please!" Papa said.

Yossi turned to him angrily. "Papa, what's the matter with you? You never used to be like this."

A shamed look passed over Papa's face. "It's different now, Yossi. If you go after him, I could get in trouble—"

"So? He deserves it—" Yossi strained against Papa's arms.

"Yossi! I could lose my job! Then what would we do?"

Yossi stopped straining. His body went slack. So that was it. That was why Papa hadn't said anything to Mr. Steiner. That was why he wouldn't let Yossi go after Steiner's son.

And with a bitter sigh, he realized that Papa was right—the family needed every single penny. If Papa lost his job, it would be a disaster.

But to be shamed so! And not to be able to fight back!

"It's not fair, Papa," Yossi said angrily.

"I know, Yossele," Papa said.

Suddenly Yossi understood what Daniel had meant the night Mrs. Belnick came, when he'd said he didn't want to take handouts from the rich owners. Especially when the owners treated them like this. And they were their own people, fellow Jews! That made it even worse.

Furiously, Yossi unfastened the toggles, threw the coat on the ground and started walking away.

"Yossi, no!" Papa cried.

"I won't wear it, Papa."

Coughing, Papa stooped to pick up the coat. "Yossi, please, it's cold."

"I don't care," Yossi said. "I'd rather freeze." Daniel's words. The other night he'd tried them out. Now he meant them.

Yossi stormed ahead, fuming. Maybe he couldn't get back at Max Steiner right now, but someday, somehow, he'd bring that Uptowner down a notch.

# Chapter Three

Papa's hand nudging his shoulder woke Yossi up. Fighting the sleepiness that he longed to give in to, he rose from his thin cotton mattress on the floor, grabbed his clothes and tiptoed into the kitchen, trying not to wake Miriam. It was still black outside. By the light of a candle, Yossi dressed quickly in the chilly room. A moment later, Daniel joined him and dressed silently.

Mama lit a fire in the coal stove and put the kettle on. Yossi shrugged on his old winter coat, trying vainly to pull the sleeves down to cover his wrists, then tugged on his woolen cap. He counted out eight pennies from a cup on the mantel and put them in his pocket, along with a hunk of rye bread. As he headed for the door, Mama whispered, "Yossi, wait. Have a cup of tea first."

Before she could say anything more, he was out the door. The first newsboy to hit the street sold his papers the quickest, Yossi knew. Tea could wait.

Although the sun had not yet risen when Yossi stepped outside, the milkman's horse clip-clopped down the street, a freight car clanged from the railyard several blocks away and a tugboat hooted on the Saint Lawrence. Montreal was waking up.

Minutes later, Yossi turned in at an office door marked *Die Zeit*. He placed the eight pennies on the counter, and a man slid a dozen Yiddish newspapers toward him. "The early bird catches the worm, eh, Mendelsohn?"

"Yes."

Yossi tucked the papers under his arm and left. Ducking his head against the wind blowing north off the river, he headed south and west, toward his corner at The Main and Des Pins. This, he was convinced, was the best corner in Montreal for selling newspapers. It was at the center of where three garment factories were located, and men streamed past from all directions on their way to work. Even the poorest could afford a penny for a paper.

Men started walking by, first a trickle, then a few more, then a flood. "Paper! Get your paper!" Yossi hollered. One by one, he sold his newspapers, pocketing twelve pennies. Four cents profit. The coins jingled satisfyingly in his pocket.

By now the sun was a faint brightening in the eastern sky. Munching on the hunk of rye bread, Yossi walked up to Rue Marie-Anne, Abie's corner.

Abie still had a couple of papers left, so Yossi kept him company until he sold them. Then the two of them set off for Steiner's Garment Works, where Abie was also a bundle carrier. His papa, Herman, worked there too.

As they walked, Abie told him about how he and Louie had been playing down at the docks the day before, and he'd found a nickel wedged between two planks.

"A whole nickel!" Yossi tried to imagine finding such riches all at once. "What'd you do with it? Go on a spending spree?"

"I gave it to Mama," Abie said. "Naomi's got a fever and she needs medicine."

Naomi was Abie's two-year-old sister. Yossi thought of her lying sick in bed and shook his head. And even if Naomi hadn't been sick, Yossi knew that Abie would have given the nickel to his mama anyway. Abie's family was even poorer than Yossi's. There were three little ones at home, and the family took in boarders to help pay the rent. They needed every penny that Abie made.

Yossi was luckier. Papa let him keep two cents of every four-cent profit he earned. Yossi had a small collection of pennies rolled up in an old sock, maybe twenty in all. He didn't know what he was saving for.

The boys turned south and a blast of wind off the river hit them. They both shivered.

"Too bad about that coat, eh?" Abie said.

Yossi shrugged, though he would have been glad of its warmth right now. "You want it?"

Abie gave him a black look. "I'm desperate, but I ain't that desperate!"

Yossi frowned. "How'm I going to get that Max Steiner back? It's got to be good. But he can't know it's me, so I don't get Papa in trouble."

Abie scratched his head. "We'll think of something, don't worry."

They turned a corner. There stood a massive brick building, four stories high, with the words STEINER'S GARMENT WORKS spelled out in yellow bricks amid the red. The two boys went to a side entrance and walked down a hallway to the packing room. There, workers were bundling pieces of cut-out cloth into piles two feet square, wrapping them in burlap and tying them with twine.

The supervisor ticked off Yossi's and Abie's

names on a list and told them where to take their deliveries. Yossi could barely hear him over the whine of the sewing machines and the rumble of the wooden tables shaking with the vibrations of many machines. Out on the floor, where Papa and Daniel worked, the noise was deafening. Sometimes Papa's ears rang all evening.

As Yossi leaned close to hear the address, Daniel's friend Solly, one of the garment packers, caught his eye and waved. When Yossi waved back, the supervisor bellowed at Solly, "Get back to work, Bregman," then cuffed Yossi's ear.

The supervisor roughly loaded the bundles onto the boys' backs. The carriers had fashioned straps that hooked over their shoulders to help carry the weight. Even so, Yossi and Abie were bent double and panting by the time they reached the end of the first block, where they parted ways.

"See you at school," Yossi called. Each day, after selling his papers and carrying his bundles, he and his pals went to the

Rebbe's for lessons. Jews weren't allowed to attend public school, and the poorer families couldn't afford a private Jewish school, so they paid the Rebbe a small fee to teach their children Hebrew, mathematics, religion, reading and writing. Yossi didn't mind—he enjoyed learning— though it was much more fun to explore the city with his friends.

Like this French section he was delivering his bundle in today. He hadn't been here before, and at first everything looked strange. There was a church on every corner, black-frocked priests swished by, and all the signs were in French. But then he noticed tumbledown tenements and shabby storefronts, ragged children picking up stray lumps of coal from the street. That wasn't strange—it was just like in his neighborhood.

From nearby, Yossi heard boys' voices, calling back and forth in French. He didn't understand much of the language—a word here or there, picked up in the shops or on the street. *"Salut"*...

"*Combien coute ça?*"—How much does it cost? Or, the phrase he heard most often, "*Va-t'en!*"—Get lost!

But today there was another sound in addition to the French words, one that Yossi didn't recognize. Sort of a scraping, then a whooshing, then a scraping again. Curious, he followed the sounds around the corner.

Between the backs of two rows of tall windowless brick tenements was a low-lying lane, covered in a treacherous sheet of ice. A group of boys, five or six of them, was on the ice. They were on skates—Yossi had seen those before, though he'd never skated himself. They were flailing away at a lump of coal. Each boy had a wooden stick, flattened on either side, with a curved end. First one boy would tap the lump with his stick, then another boy would push away the first boy's stick with his own and send the coal in the opposite direction. Then another boy would capture the lump and skate away with it, pushing it forward with his stick.

With each move, the boys shouted to one another, cheering and laughing.

Back and forth they skated, up and down the sheet of ice, zigzagging from side to side, darting around one another, always chasing the elusive lump of coal. As they stopped and turned, their skates made sharp rasping sounds and the blades sent up showers of ice flakes. Sometimes a boy fell, but he sprang to his feet, unhurt, and sped off again.

Yossi stood entranced. Heedless of the weight on his back, of the cold, he watched the beautiful game.

Then one of the players, a tall agile boy with blond hair sticking out below his blue knitted cap, gave a mighty thrust with his stick and sent the lump of coal soaring down the ice. It flew past a boy Yossi hadn't even noticed before, a burly fellow in a red stocking cap, who stood in front of a large barricade of snow. The red-capped boy flung up his stick to try to bat the lump away, but he was too late. The coal sailed past his shoulder and lodged in the snowbank.

Grinning, the blond boy threw both arms in the air, stick raised, and shouted, *"But!"* as the red-hatted fellow rapped his stick on the ice in disgust.

Without quite understanding what had happened, only knowing it was wonderful, Yossi grinned too.

As the blond boy turned, laughing, toward his teammates, he spotted Yossi. He stopped and stared. Not smiling. Not frowning. Just looking at Yossi, at the bundle on his back.

Yossi's grin faded. The boy didn't look friendly, and neither did his mates, who also stopped and stared, grouping themselves around the blond boy as if waiting for him to make a move.

Yossi stood still. After all, they were French. Which meant they were Catholic. Everyone knew that the Catholics hated the Jews because they believed that the Jews had killed Christ. It wasn't true, of course, but that didn't stop them from believing it.

But in spite of the French boys' unfriendly

looks, Yossi couldn't help himself. Sweeping his arm toward the ice, he called out, in Yiddish, "What is it?"

The blond boy waved his stick in the air. Thinking the boy meant to chase him away, Yossi turned and started trudging down the street. But a moment later, he heard a shout: *"Le hockey!"*

Yossi whipped around. The boy was still looking at him, stick raised. Yossi flashed him a smile. He couldn't be sure, but he thought the other boy smiled back. "Hockey," Yossi whispered to himself as he hurried down the street to make his delivery.

Twenty minutes later, free of his bundle, Yossi raced up the stairs to the flat and burst in the door. Sadie was already at work at the sewing machine, and Miriam and Mama were hand-stitching by the window.

Mama leaped to her feet.

"Yossi, where were you?" she said. "You'll be late for your lessons. What will the Rebbe say?"

"Mama!" Yossi said excitedly. "I saw these boys. Frenchies. Playing a game. Hockey, it's called. And I'm going to learn how to play it, Mama."

"And you haven't even had breakfast yet," Mama fussed.

"Hockey," Yossi repeated dreamily. He gulped a cup of tea and grabbed a roll and a hunk of cheese. Then he strapped on his book bag.

But before he left, he carefully counted ten pennies into the jar on the mantel and added two to his collection in the rolled-up sock.

Finally he knew what he was saving for.

A pair of skates.

# Chapter Four

One day, when Mama and Papa and Sadie were out, Yossi pulled the rolled-up sock out from under his pallet and emptied it onto his blanket. Thirty-two pennies. The cheapest pair of ice skates he could find cost two dollars. Making two cents a day on the papers, plus another one or two cents for lugging the bundles, it would take him at least a month and a half to save up the rest of the money. It was mid-January already. The ice might be gone by then!

With a groan, Yossi put the money back in the sock. So long to wait! He'd just have to figure out another way to make money, that was all. But how?

His stomach growled. He couldn't think on an empty stomach. He wandered into the kitchen to see if there was anything to eat.

As he approached, he heard giggling, then silence, then more giggling. He peered about. There was a small alcove next to the kitchen, where Mama kept the broom and mop and wash bucket. Squeezed into the alcove, flattened against the broom and mop handles, practically standing in the bucket, were Miriam and Daniel. Daniel's arms were around Miriam's waist, Miriam's arms were around Daniel's neck, and they were kissing.

"Yuch!" Yossi shouted. "That is disgusting!"

Miriam and Daniel broke apart, looking startled. Then Miriam smiled mischievously. "What is, Yossi?"

Yossi made a face. "All that…kissing."

They both laughed. Miriam pulled Daniel's face toward her. "You mean like this, Yossi?" She smacked Daniel on the lips.

Yossi covered his eyes. "Ugh! Don't do that!"

Miriam and Daniel giggled. Ignoring him, they started kissing again, with loud, slurping sounds that Yossi was sure they were making on purpose.

"I mean it, you two! I can't watch. I can't eat. Why don't you get married and get your own place? Do your kissing there!"

Daniel and Miriam broke apart. The teasing was gone from Daniel's face. "Don't you think that's exactly what we want, Yossi?" he said. Miriam stepped forward. Her face was red and her hands were clenched. "Don't you think that's all we long for? To get married and have a place of our own."

Yossi was stunned—by the misery in Miriam's eyes, the fury on Daniel's face. "Then—why don't you?"

"Because we can't afford it!" Miriam said.

"Because on the miserable wages that thief Steiner pays, I can't support a wife. I can't start a family!" Daniel shouted.

"'That thief Steiner?'" Yossi repeated. "What do you mean, Daniel? He doesn't steal from us."

"Yes, he does," Daniel shot back. "When we spend our lives making him rich—"

"And our pockets are still empty—," Miriam added.

"And he lives like a king—"

"While we go hungry and cold—"

"I call that stealing!" Daniel said.

Yossi thought about the grand houses he'd seen that Shabbas morning. He thought about Mr. Steiner with his gold watch chain and Max Steiner in his fancy new coat. He thought about himself and his family in their threadbare clothes, trying to stretch their pennies so they could pay the rent each month.

"But...it's not right," Yossi said.

"Of course it's not right!" Daniel said.

Just then the front door opened and Papa, Mama and Sadie came in, brushing snow from their coats and stamping their boots. "What's all this, then?" Mama looked surprised.

41

"Yossi wants to know why Daniel and I don't get married and move into our own flat," Miriam said bitterly.

Sadie sighed. "Money. Always money."

"It's not that we're not trying to save, Mama!" Daniel said. "It's that the owners don't pay enough. A worker can barely keep body and soul together, let alone make a better life. We need a living wage, not starvation pay!"

At the word "starvation," Yossi thought of Abie, of how his family was always hungry. Then Yossi thought of Mr. Steiner's well-padded middle.

"*Nu?*" Papa said, coughing. "So what can you do?"

"Organize!" Daniel shouted. "I keep telling you, Avram, it's the only way. The workers have to pull together and demand higher wages."

" 'Demand,' " Papa repeated with a harsh laugh. "Make demands of Saul Steiner?"

"Then we have to refuse to work until he agrees," Daniel said.

"Strike?" Mama said, aghast.

42

"What's a strike?" Yossi asked.

"It's when the workers refuse to work until the owners give them what they want," Daniel said.

"You'll get your head bashed in!" Mama said.

"You'll get thrown in jail," Papa added.

"It'll be worth it," Daniel said.

"Daniel!" Sadie exclaimed.

"Agitation is not the way," Papa said. He paused, wracked by coughing. "Better we should sit down with Mr. Steiner, talk like reasonable people—"

"Reasonable!" Daniel interrupted him. "Avram, we could talk until we were blue in the face and he'd never listen. All Steiner's interested in—he and the other owners—is profit. You think he'll pay you a higher wage if you ask him nicely? Not if it cuts into his profit."

"Surely if he understood how badly off the workers are, how hard it is to support a family—," Sadie began.

"He knows, Mama, he just doesn't care," Daniel said. "The only way is to form unions—not just at Steiner's, but at all the sweatshops—and demand higher wages."

"And better conditions," Miriam added. "Forcing people to work twelve, fifteen hours a day—it's criminal!"

"Miriam!" Papa said, then went into a spasm of coughing.

Miriam's face turned red but she didn't stop. "Well, it is, Papa! Why do you think you have that cough? It's from the garment dust. But will they put in fans to blow it out? No!"

Yossi looked at his sister in amazement. He'd never heard her speak out like this.

"You're picking up crazy ideas from him," Papa said to Miriam, pointing at Daniel.

"Crazy? You know what's crazy, Papa? Putting up with it," Miriam said. "Daniel's right. The owners will keep taking advantage of us unless we get organized and stand up for our rights."

"My daughter, a socialist," Mama said, shaking her head.

"What's a socialist?" Yossi said.

"Someone who believes in workers' rights," Miriam answered.

"Someone who makes trouble," Papa said. He turned to Daniel. "You know Steiner won't stand for it. You'll lose your job—and then what? You'll have nothing."

"I have nothing now, Avram," Daniel said bitterly. "I love your daughter and I want to marry her. We work as hard as we can. We save every penny. And still I can't support her. Do you know how that makes me feel?"

Yossi thought he knew how it made Daniel feel—just the way he'd felt when Max Steiner taunted him.

"And it's going to go on and on, unless we do something about it," Daniel continued. "I've been talking to workers at the other sweatshops, and they all agree. The owners have to change—and we have to make them."

"Don't be crazy, Daniel!" Papa said. "It's dangerous, getting mixed up in labor agitation. You'll bring trouble down on all of us!"

The two of them stood nose to nose. "I'll be careful, Avram," Daniel said, more softly, "but I won't stop struggling—"

Miriam took his hand. "We'll struggle together."

"And we'll win," Daniel said.

There was a silence.

"And then you and Miriam can get married and do your kissing somewhere else," Yossi said, and everyone laughed.

Yossi grinned, glad to have broken the tension. But as he left the room, he wondered what danger Papa was talking about. And he wondered what it would take for Daniel and Miriam to win.

# Chapter Five

Arm in arm, Yossi, Abie, Benny, Louie and Milton skipped down the street, kicking up little mounds of fresh snow. The Rebbe had been called away to sit with a sick relative, so they had an afternoon free of lessons.

Benny started humming "My Rumania, My Rumania," a popular Yiddish song, and soon the others joined in, singing loudly. When women on the street wagged their fingers, the boys burst into laughter and sang louder.

They strolled down several streets of tenements, then turned onto a street of shops past Rosen's, the chemist's...

Abramowitz's Dry Goods...Fogelman's Kosher Butcher. They stopped, gazing at the huge joints of kosher meat that hung in the window, turning slowly on strings.

Yossi's mouth watered. "I bet I could eat that whole roast," he said, pointing to one large piece.

Abie sighed. "Last time I had meat—real brisket, not just scraps—was Rosh Hashanah."

Four months ago, Yossi thought. Poor Abie. At least Yossi's family wasn't quite so badly off. Once in a while, Mama and Sadie were able to pool their pennies and buy a chicken, or even a piece of meat, for Shabbas dinner.

"Mmmm...can't you just smell it, a beautiful roast, all brown on the outside and pink on the inside?" Louie said.

"And roasted potatoes, crisp and crackling...," Milton added.

"Oh...," Abie groaned, "I can taste it."

Yossi turned away from the window. "Stop! This is torture. Come on, let's get something we *can* afford."

He led them to a pickled herring cart around the corner. Moishe, a young man with a drooping brown mustache, stood behind the cart, shuffling from one foot to the other and clapping his mittened hands to keep warm. When he saw the boys, he smiled. "Good afternoon, young gentlemen. What can I do for you?"

*Two Herrings a Penny*, said the sign.

Yossi hesitated. There were five of them. They had enough money for two servings, but not three. Oh well, he'd go without. "Four herrings, please," he said.

"Certainly." Moishe ladeled four small fish onto a piece of parchment paper, then, glancing at the boys, added another to the pile. "Two pennies, please."

"But—"

"That's all right." He smiled and the sides of his mustache rose like wings. "One little herring I can spare."

Yossi paid him, vowing to himself that he'd repay him the extra penny. Moishe, he knew, had two babies at home, and even a penny made a difference when you had so little.

The boys wolfed down the herrings, licking their fingers. They were leaving when a voice cried, "Yossi Mendelsohn, is that you?"

Yossi turned. A thin young man with pale watery eyes and straw-like brown hair was approaching. "Hello, Jonah," he said without enthusiasm.

"What are you doing here? Why aren't you at lessons?"

"The Rebbe gave us the afternoon off. What are you doing here?"

Jonah's eyes shifted from side to side. "Oh, just doing an errand for one of the supervisors. They rely on me, you know. Give me special jobs. Run here, run there." He gave an oily smile. "Well, I'd better get back to work. There's a new shipment of wool coming in today. Very big, very important. But then, you boys wouldn't know about such things." With a smug expression, he waved goodbye.

"Who's that?" Milton said when he was gone.

"Jonah Fishkin," Yossi answered.

"Something fishy about *him*," Louie said, and the others chuckled.

"I don't like that fellow," Benny said. "He thinks he knows everything."

Abie frowned. "At Steiner's, he's always hanging around the supervisors, like he's better than the workers."

"Trying to get in good with Steiner, probably," Louie said.

"That reminds me," Yossi said. "How am I going to get back at that rotten son of his?"

They had been making their way north, away from the waterfront, into a better neighborhood. Somewhere in the distance, a church bell pealed, three long rings and one short one.

"Three-thirty," Milton said. "You know, Max Steiner and his rich friends go to the fancy new Jewish school. They'll be getting off in half an hour. We could ambush them and attack them with snowballs."

"He deserves worse than a measly snowball," Yossi grumbled. "But it's better than nothing. Let's go."

The boys started making their way toward the school. As they walked down an alley behind a grocer's store, a man in a white apron came out the back door, holding a basket. A moment later, a putrid smell hit their nostrils.

"Phew! What's that?" Yossi said.

"Rotten eggs," the storekeeper replied, frowning. Lifting the basket above a wooden crate full of garbage, he started to upend it.

Yossi's eyes lit up. "Wait! I think we can take those off your hands, sir."

Abie gaped at him. "Have you lost your mind, Yossi?"

"Good riddance," the shopkeeper said, handing the basket to Yossi before he went back inside.

The others stared at Yossi. "What on earth do you want with a bunch of rotten eggs?" Louie asked.

Yossi grinned. "Ammunition, boys."

Yossi had them take off their caps and, very gingerly, fill them with eggs. They walked to the edge of the school grounds, lay down behind a snowbank and waited.

When the bell tolled four, the front doors opened and boys started spilling out. Boys in smart winter coats and warm caps. Boys wearing leather boots. Well-fed boys with chubby rosy cheeks.

"Now, remember," Yossi whispered to the others, "Max Steiner is mine."

After a while, Yossi heard a familiar voice. He peered over the snowbank. Sure enough, it was Max and his cronies.

"You should see my new ice skates," Max was saying. "Papa says they're the most expensive skates in Montreal. They go like lightning!"

"I have new skates too," one of the other boys said.

"Not as good as mine," Max snapped. "Mine are the best you can buy."

Yossi raised a finger. "Now," he whispered.

The boys let fly. *Pow*! *Bam*! *Splat*! The eggs went sailing. Some smashed on the ground. Some spattered on arms or

backs. A rotten stench hung in the air like a cloud.

"Wha'—?"

"Yuch!"

"Phew! It stinks!"

The startled boys ran every which way.

Yossi took careful aim. His egg landed right in the middle of Max's chest. Orange yolk and slimy white started oozing down the front of his new coat.

Keeping hidden, Yossi peeked over the snowbank. Max was jumping up and down, flailing his arms, wriggling in disgust. "Ugh! Phew! Aagghh! Get it off me!"

Yossi laughed to himself. How he longed to taunt Max Steiner as Max had taunted him! But he didn't dare, in case Max found out who it was and Papa got in trouble.

Quickly, before Max and the other boys could climb over the snowbank to see who their attackers were, Yossi gave a signal. He and his friends ran away, disappearing around the corner so quickly, it was as if they had never been there at all.

# Chapter Six

Papa's cough got worse. At first he coughed only when he exerted himself, like when he climbed the stairs or walked in the cold. Then he coughed whenever he spoke. Soon he was coughing all the time.

The cough changed from a wet rattle to a dry wracking cough that shook his body. All night Yossi lay stiff and tense on his mattress, listening to Papa's violent hacking, and in the morning he was nearly as tired as Papa was.

"Send for the doctor, Avram," Mama said.

Papa shook his head. "We can't afford it. It'll pass." He coughed again.

Then Papa began to run a fever. His eyes were glazed. He had no energy, no appetite. He dragged himself to work. He dragged himself back.

One day he couldn't get out of bed. He raised his head, gave a shuddering cough, and fell back. Mama motioned to Yossi. "Go for Dr. Rosenthal."

"We can't afford it," Papa rasped.

"We'll afford it!" she scolded. "I can't afford to lose you!"

Yossi ran.

Dr. Rosenthal listened to Papa's chest. He took his pulse, felt his neck and looked down his throat. "Pneumonia," he pronounced. He looked at Papa. "You're a garment worker, right?"

Papa looked surprised. "How did you know?"

"I see it all the time. Starts as an irritation from the dust and stale air, then grows into an infection." Dr. Rosenthal shook his head. "Those sweatshops are breeding grounds for illness."

Papa flapped his hand as if dismissing

Dr. Rosenthal's words, but Yossi remembered what Miriam had said about Mr. Steiner refusing to put in fans. And now Papa had gotten sick from working at the sweatshop!

Dr. Rosenthal turned to Mama. "Plenty of liquids—tea, chicken broth, juice if you can get it. Sponge baths for the fever. And—," he turned to Papa with a stern look, "—complete bed rest. No work until the fever and cough are completely gone."

"How long?" Papa whispered.

"However long it takes," Dr. Rosenthal said as he left.

The next morning, Papa was up at the usual hour.

"What do you think you're doing?" Mama cried.

"Going to work."

"The doctor said bed rest!"

"We can't afford for me to miss work." He coughed, his shoulders shaking. "I'll be all right."

"Get back in bed this minute!"

Papa ignored her and headed down the stairs.

An hour later, Yossi was at Steiner's delivering a bundle of finished garments. There was a commotion on the other side of the packing room door, and a man bustled through. "Worker collapsed out there. The boss ain't happy."

Yossi ran through the door before the supervisor could stop him. Papa lay on the floor beside his sewing machine. Daniel was cradling his head. Yossi helped Daniel sit Papa up. He was trembling and his skin was burning hot. They helped Papa to his feet. As they walked him out of the sweatshop, one of Papa's arms draped over Daniel's shoulders and the other over Yossi's, Mr. Steiner was bellowing at the workers, who'd stopped their machines to watch, "What are you staring at? Get back to work!"

Yossi and Daniel half-carried Papa home and laid him in his bed. Now, Yossi thought, Papa had no choice but to follow Dr. Rosenthal's instructions.

Over the next several days, Yossi carried extra bundles to earn a few more pennies. Every chance he got, coming or going from Steiner's, he went by the ice rink where the French boys were playing hockey.

They continued to ignore him. Well, not exactly ignore. They looked at him— curiously, Yossi thought. But they didn't call hello or invite him to join them.

Yossi didn't know whether it was because he didn't speak French, or because he was Jewish—everyone knew that most of the boys who carried bundles were Jews— or because, since they had skates, they thought they were better than he was.

He didn't care. He'd paid back Moishe, the herring vendor, and still his stash of pennies was growing. With all the extra bundles he was carrying, the sock under his mattress was positively bulging. Any day now, he'd have enough to buy a pair of skates. He'd make friends with the French boys somehow. And then he'd learn to play the glorious game of hockey.

Meanwhile, Papa was still sick. Even a few days after he'd collapsed, he was still running a fever, alternately shivering and sweating. He slept fitfully, thrashing in his sleep, and when he was awake, he coughed constantly.

Mama walked around with a deep crease in her forehead. She was in and out of the bedroom all day, feeling Papa's forehead, wiping him down with cool cloths, trying to get him to drink water, tea, soup. When she wasn't fussing over him, she was sewing. She and Miriam and Sadie were all working from early in the morning until late at night, trying to make up for Papa's lost wages.

After several days, Papa was able to sit up and take a little soup, but he was still coughing constantly and the fever came and went. The next day his fever was lower, but he was still too weak to get out of bed. A couple of days later, the fever broke. Color started coming back into his face.

The sharp line in Mama's forehead faded and she went back to scolding. "If you'd sent for the doctor when I told you to! But no, he has to be the hero. 'It'll pass,' he says. Fah!" All this, while feeding Papa and wiping his chin.

Yossi breathed a sigh of relief.

A couple of days later, Yossi came home with four pennies jingling in his pocket. He'd carried four bundles that day. It was time to count his money. He must have enough by now!

He opened the door to the sound of yelling. Mama had her coat and scarf on and her cloth market bag over her arm, turnip greens poking out the top. Papa also had his coat on—over his pajamas. The coal scuttle was on the floor, over-turned, coal spilling in a dusty black flood. Papa was leaning over, hands on his knees, coughing.

"Two minutes I go out to do some mar-keting and you sneak out of bed!" Mama scolded.

"Didn't...sneak...," Papa said, between rasping coughs.

"What were you thinking?" Mama shrilled, putting down her bag.

"...wanted to bring up some coal...," Papa rasped. "...Daniel and Yossi doing all the work..."

"Papa!" Yossi said. "I don't mind. You shouldn't—"

"Listen to your son. He's smarter than you!" Mama snapped. "Up and down the stairs in the cold...not even out of your sickbed yet..." As she hollered, she took off Papa's coat, put his old sweater around his shoulders and led him into the bedroom.

"I feel useless," Papa grumbled.

"Useless! I'll give you useless. You'll be useless if you work yourself into an early grave!" Mama felt his forehead. "*Oy vey*, he's burning up. Quick, Yossi, some cool wet cloths."

While Mama rubbed him down, Yossi cleaned up the spilled coal and filled the scuttle again. Mama came out of the bedroom. The furrow was back in her forehead.

That night, as he was getting ready for bed, Yossi felt the four pennies in his pocket. He'd forgotten all about them. He reached for his sock, but then stopped. He gazed at Papa, who was sleeping. His cheeks were hollow beneath his gaunt cheekbones. Yossi could hear the wheeze in his chest as he struggled to breathe.

Yossi tiptoed from the room. Mama was in the kitchen, hand-sewing a lacy collar on a lady's blouse, squinting in the candlelight. Yossi sat beside her.

"Papa's not going to be able to go back to work for a while, is he, Mama?"

She looked at him. "No, Yossi. Why?"

"No reason. Just wondering."

Later, Yossi lay in bed, waiting for Mama to fall asleep. When he heard her slow breathing, he reached under his mattress, pulled out his sock and tiptoed into the kitchen. Quietly, he counted his savings into the cup on the mantel. One dollar and seventy-six cents.

Not quietly enough. Mama tiptoed over just as he was putting in the last penny.

"Yossi, what are you doing?" she whispered. She looked in the cup. "Your money! I can't take it."

"It's all right, Mama. You need it more than I do."

"But Yossi—"

"Take it, Mama."

She looked at him with shining eyes. Then she threw her arms around him. "Oh, Yossi! Thank you."

Yossi hugged her back. He didn't mind, really he didn't. He was proud to help.

But oh, his skates!

# Chapter Seven

Daniel was busy. Careful not to let Papa see, he scribbled on scraps of paper, then burned them. Sometimes, Yossi noticed, he arrived home late, famished and exhausted, his eyes burning with some inner fire. Other times, he came home, wolfed down his dinner, then hurried out again.

Once, Yossi saw Daniel standing in a tenement doorway talking to Solly, the friendly fellow who bundled up the garment pieces.

Another time, Yossi saw Daniel come out of a building followed by Jonah Fishkin. Jonah was leaning close to Daniel. His face had a crafty expression, though his pale eyes blinked innocently. Yossi remembered what Abie had said about Jonah hanging around the supervisors. So what was he doing with Daniel? Did that mean Jonah was involved with the workers too? That was odd. He'd have to ask Daniel, Yossi thought.

Whatever Daniel was up to, Miriam was mixed up in it too. Yossi often saw them whispering together. Sometimes she even went with Daniel to the meetings—much to Mama's disapproval.

One evening when Miriam was tying on her headscarf, Mama scolded her, "What do you think you're doing, young lady, running out after dark, getting involved in labor meetings and unions and God knows what? It's not proper!"

Miriam buttoned her coat. "I'm fighting for a better world, Mama—so my children, God willing, won't have to live like this."

Mama couldn't argue with that.

The next morning, as Yossi was leaving to pick up his newspapers, Daniel followed him down the stairs. Glancing right and left, he said in a low voice, "Yossele, I need your help. I shouldn't drag you into this, but...I don't know what else to do."

"Sure, Daniel," Yossi said. "What?"

"Let's walk," Daniel said, and they strolled down the street. Daniel looked around to make sure no one was near. "Listen, Yossi. One of our comrades, Solly—you know him, he works in the packing room—"

Yossi nodded.

"Well, his brother-in-law works in a print shop, and we've had him print up some handbills urging the men to form a union—not just at Steiner's but at all three sweatshops in the neighborhood. Solly's going to bring them to work today. But I don't want him to give them to me because—"

He broke off, waiting until a pair of workers, heading toward them, had passed by.

"Because I know they're watching me. So..." He hesitated, then plunged on.

"Would you take the packet instead, Yossi? No one suspects you. Stuff it in your bundle, hide it under your shirt, whatever you like. Take it home and give it to Miriam. She'll take care of it. What do you say?"

"Sure!" Yossi said.

"Not so loud," Daniel whispered, looking around. "Listen, Yossi, this isn't a game. It's serious. You could get into real trouble. Your papa would kill me if he knew I'd dragged you into it."

Yossi thought for a moment. Was this what Papa had meant when he talked about danger? Yossi didn't understand exactly what unions were all about, but he did know that Papa would disapprove if Yossi got involved. And that Yossi would get into a heap of trouble if he were caught. But he also thought that Daniel and Miriam were right to fight for the workers.

And besides, he thought with only a twinge of guilt, he wasn't doing anything much, just taking a little packet. Papa would never know, and no one would get in trouble.

"Don't worry, Daniel, Papa won't find out. I'll be as sneaky as anything."

"All right, then." Daniel grinned. "Thanks, Yossi. You're a real comrade."

Giving Yossi a hearty pat on the back, he veered off toward Steiner's. Yossi headed down the hill to the *Die Zeit* office. He stood tall. Comrade Yossi! A friend of the workers!

An hour later, Yossi's heart was pounding as he entered Steiner's packing room. A thought had just crossed his mind. What if he ended up with one of the other workers' bundles, instead of Solly's? How would he get the packet? Solly might have to give it to Daniel after all, and Daniel might get caught, and...

But in the end, everything went like clockwork. When the supervisor was looking the other way, Solly reached under his shirt, laid something on top of the pile and quickly covered it with several pieces of fabric. He cut a length of burlap, wrapped and tied the bundle, then jerked his head at Yossi. "You there," he said as if Yossi were just another delivery boy, "take this to Mrs. Jablonsky and be quick about it." But he patted Yossi's shoulder as he hoisted the bundle onto Yossi's back.

When Yossi turned around, he was surprised to see Jonah Fishkin in the packing room. What was he doing there?

"Why, it's young Yossi Mendelsohn," Jonah said in an unnaturally friendly voice.

Yossi ignored him, edging out of the room with an uneasy feeling. Then, when he opened the packing room door, who should be standing in the hallway but Max Steiner. What was *he* doing there?

Yossi quickly passed him by, his mind churning. Could Max have figured out that it was Yossi who had thrown the eggs?

He glanced back then, and what he saw froze him—Max, Jonah and the supervisor whispering together. And behind them, a panic-stricken look on his face, Solly motioning Yossi to *go!*

Yossi went. Darting out the factory door, he half-ran, half-shuffled down the street, the bundle bouncing on his back. When he reached the corner, he looked back. Max and the supervisor were just coming out of the building. Yossi whipped around the corner, nearly knocking over a woman pushing a baby carriage, then took off down the street, dodging passersby, the bundle jouncing from side to side.

That dirty rat Jonah! Yossi thought. Jonah must have learned about the handbills from Daniel and told Max Steiner so he could tell his papa. With a pang of guilt, Yossi realized that he'd forgotten to tell Daniel what Abie had said about Jonah.

The shouts of "Stop!" and "Get him!" grew closer and closer. Yossi knew that Max and the supervisor would soon be upon him. For a moment he thought of dropping the bundle and running away—but even if he saved his own skin, they'd find the packet, and that would mean trouble for everyone. Yossi reached another corner and glanced back. They were less than a block away. Winded, he glanced around, seeking an escape. The grocer's where they'd got the rotten eggs! It was up ahead, and Yossi remembered there was an alley behind it. He darted into the narrow passageway between the grocer's and the shop next door, and turned into the alley. The wooden crate behind the grocer's was overflowing with spoiled vegetables, rotten fruit, sawdust and broken eggs. Wedging himself between the back of the building and the crate, Yossi crouched down, his nose filling with putrid smells.

Footsteps pounded up the passageway, then thundered past his hiding place. "Where'd he go?" the supervisor yelled.

"I know he came this way," Max said, walking right past the crate.

The supervisor paced back and forth. "Well, there's no sign of him."

"But I saw him—"

"Phew! It stinks!" the supervisor said. "Come on, let's go."

They disappeared down the passageway.

When their footsteps had faded, Yossi eased out from behind the crate. He snuck through the passageway and looked down the street. Max and the supervisor were a block away. Yossi turned in the opposite direction, running as quickly as he could, reaching back with both hands to steady the bundle. He'd gone half a block when he heard, "There he is! Get him!"

They must have turned around and seen him! Panting, zigzagging from street to street, not sure where he was, Yossi ran...ran.... Turning down an alley, he found himself at the ice rink. And there were the French boys, skating back and forth, sticks in hand.

"Help!" Yossi cried in Yiddish, then sank to his knees at the edge of the ice.

The tall blond boy—the one who'd told Yossi the name of the game—skated over. The other boys gathered around.

"Bundle...packet...," Yossi panted in Yiddish, pointing to his load. "Steiner's... they're coming..." He looked over his shoulder fearfully. "Hide me!" He put his arms over his head. *"S'il vous plait!"* he added desperately, hoping he'd got the words right.

For a long moment the blond boy stared at Yossi. He peered up the street. Then he sprang into action. Speaking rapidly to the others in French, he beckoned toward the end of the rink, where the burly boy in the red stocking cap was standing in front of the snowbank. The burly boy skated over. The blond boy ripped the bundle from Yossi's back and handed it to the burly boy, who was quickly joined by two others. Digging with their hockey sticks, they quickly hollowed out a space in the snowbank, shoved the bundle into it and covered it with snow.

The blond boy led Yossi across the ice, holding Yossi's elbow as his booted feet slipped and slid. He thrust Yossi in front of the snowbank and switched Yossi's woven cap with the red stocking cap of the burly boy. He shoved the boy's stick into Yossi's hands. Shouting something at the others, he batted the lump of coal down the ice. The game resumed, just as Max and the supervisor came running down the street.

Leaning on the stick for balance, Yossi watched the two visitors out of the corner of his eye.

"Not again," Max cried, stamping his foot.

"Where is he?" the supervisor said.

"He can't have just disappeared!"

The supervisor shrugged. Edging closer to the ice, he called in a mixture of Yiddish and English, "You boys! Did you see a boy go by? With a big bundle on his back?" He gestured to indicate the bundle.

The boys shrugged and shook their heads as if they had no idea what he was talking about. They continued their game, zooming up and down the ice. The blond boy got control of the lump of coal and started skating toward Yossi.

*Don't come near me!* Yossi thought, panicked. *They'll see me!* But then he realized that if the boys purposely stayed away from him, it would look even more suspicious.

The blond boy advanced, pushing the lump with first one side of his stick and then the other. One short brown-haired fellow raced him for the coal with quick, choppy steps, but the blond boy was too fast. Pulling back with his stick, the blond boy looked up and his eyes locked with Yossi's. In that moment, Yossi forgot about the bundle and the packet and the danger—forgot about everything except what he had to do, which was to stop the blond boy from getting the lump of coal past him. He lowered his stick to the ice, keeping his eye on the coal. The blond boy fired. The lump rose into the air. Realizing his mistake, Yossi started bringing his stick up. Too late. The lump of coal sailed over his shoulder, into the snowbank.

*"But!"* the blond boy called. Cheers erupted. The blond boy slid into the

snowbank, stick raised, knocking Yossi off his feet and toppling both of them onto the ice.

"Those stupid Frenchies," Yossi heard Max say.

"Come on, we're wasting our time," the supervisor said.

When Yossi looked up, they were walking away.

Lying on the ice, Yossi found himself face to face with the blond boy. Blue eyes stared into brown. Yossi grinned. The other boy grinned back, revealing a chipped tooth.

"Yossi," Yossi said, pointing to himself.

"René," the other boy said.

Yossi pushed himself to his knees. He grasped René's arm. "Thanks!" he said in Yiddish.

René clasped Yossi's hand. "*De rien*," he said. Yossi couldn't understand the words, but he knew that René was saying that it was all right.

The two boys got to their feet, and the others gathered around. René introduced

Yossi, then presented the other boys to him. Michel, the stocky boy who'd traded places with Yossi. Jean-Paul, the quick brown-haired boy. Hugo, a tall boy with a dimpled chin. Georges and Jacques, freckled boys who appeared to be twins.

All of them slapped Yossi on the back—except the boy named Hugo. He kept a little apart from the others and looked at Yossi warily.

René gestured down the street at the departing pair. He spat on the ice. *"Les maudits Anglais."*

Michel rubbed his fingers together to indicate money. *"Les riches Anglais."*

The other boys nodded, and so did Yossi, getting the meaning.

"My papa," Yossi said in Yiddish. "Steiner's." He mimed someone hunched over a sewing machine, pushing cloth through.

*"Oui, mon papa aussi,"* Jean-Paul said, gesturing to himself.

*"Notre maman,"* Georges said, mimicking

someone sewing tiny stiches with a needle and thread.

"Yes!" Yossi cried. "My mama too. And my sister." He squinted as if to show how hard the sewing was on the eyes.

"*Oui, oui,*" Jacques said, rubbing his eyes.

Yossi sighed. So his family, and his friends' families, weren't the only ones toiling for the garment bosses. He'd seen the run-down houses in the French neighborhood—now he knew why these boys were as poor as he was.

That reminded him of the bundle. Hastily, he dug away at the snowbank with the stick and pulled it out. Then he hoisted the slightly damp bundle onto his back.

"Good–bye—and thanks," he called.

"*Salut,*" the boys called.

Bent over, Yossi started walking away.

"*Attends!*" Michel yelled. Yossi turned back. Quickly Michel traded caps with him.

With a wave, Yossi left.

# Chapter Eight

Slowly Papa got better. With Yossi's money, Mama had bought a chicken for soup and herbs for tea and even a precious lemon and some honey, and she fed Papa bowlfuls and cupfuls until he protested he was going to float away. Soon he began to eat a little more, sleep a little less. He started sitting up in bed, then sitting in a chair, then walking around the flat. At first, when he tried going up and down the stairs, he leaned on the banister and hacked. Mama said he wasn't ready to go back to work.

But soon he was able to climb the stairs with only a slight wheeze.

"See?" he said.

"Not yet," Mama said.

He began following her around the flat, poking into her cooking, her cleaning, her sewing.

"Go, already!" Mama said.

So he went back to work.

Daniel and Miriam continued their whispered conversations, their secret meetings. They tried to hide their activities from Papa, but Yossi was sure that Papa knew what was going on. Pretending to brush the snow from his boots, Papa lingered by the door when they were whispering on the other side. One time, when they were out, Yossi saw him take a handbill from under Miriam's mattress. Yossi expected him to crumple it in disgust, but instead he looked at it thoughtfully.

That was interesting, Yossi thought. He realized that ever since Papa had gotten over his pneumonia, he didn't have such a disapproving look on his face anymore. He'd stopped arguing with Miriam and

Daniel. And once, after they'd gone out yet again, Papa said to Mama, "Those two hotheads." Yossi could have sworn there was a touch of pride in his voice.

Maybe, Yossi thought, Papa was beginning to change his mind.

It grew colder. At the street corners, snow was piled up to Yossi's waist. In the mornings, when he stood on his corner selling *Die Zeit*, the wind seemed to blow right through his old coat. More than once, Yossi thought longingly of Max Steiner's almost-new coat. It was still in the trunk at the foot of Mama and Papa's bed; they hadn't given it away. Still hoping he'd change his mind, no doubt. Standing on the corner, shivering, Yossi thought of the gloating look on Max's face when he'd taunted him. Yossi pulled his old coat tighter. He'd never wear Steiner's coat. Never!

Yossi stopped by the ice rink every chance he got. On his way from selling his newspapers to Steiner's. On his way from

Steiner's to deliver the bundles. On his way home from lessons.

He stood at the end of the ice and watched. He studied the boys' moves. He learned the game. He saw how René passed the lump of coal, not to where Jean-Paul was right then, but to where Jean-Paul would be in three strides. He saw how Jacques pretended to shoot the lump, making Michel move his stick, and then, once Michel was out of the way, buried the lump in the snowbank.

Yossi learned that the game of hockey was not really played with a lump of coal, but with a flat rubber disc called *une rondelle de hockey*. And that you didn't really shoot the *rondelle* into a snowbank, but into an upright net called *un filet*. And that there were five players for each team on the ice at a time, plus a goaltender— Michel's position—at either end.

Yossi longed for the day when he had his skates and could play with René and the other boys. But now, after having given Mama and Papa his pennies, he was starting to save all over again—and his skates seemed further away than ever.

Yossi learned a few French words. Then a few more. He taught the French boys some Yiddish words. They all began to speak a mixture of French and Yiddish, with grunts and facial expressions and panto-mime thrown in when words failed.

With this mixed language, Yossi learned that most of the boys' fathers, and many of their older brothers too, worked all winter cutting down trees in the woods, far from home. It was dangerous work, the boys told him. Some of their fathers were missing fingers.

"My papa's leg got crushed," Jean-Paul said. He limped several steps to show Yossi. "That's why he works at Steiner's." He frowned. "But that miser pays so little, our family is in a bad way."

Yossi put his hand on Jean-Paul's shoulder. "Our family too."

All the French boys were friendly to

Yossi—all except Hugo. He never greeted Yossi, never smiled at him. When the other boys practiced their Yiddish, Hugo didn't join in. When the boys skated over to the side of the rink to say hello to Yossi, Hugo stayed put.

One day, Yossi brought Abie, Benny, Louie and Milton to meet the French boys and see the glorious game he'd been telling them about. The two groups crowded together, pointing and gesturing as they exchanged names.

All but Hugo. He kept himself apart, glancing darkly at Yossi's pals. Yossi heard him say something under his breath about *"les Juifs."*

Yossi knew those words: The Jews. He turned to Hugo, hands on hips. "What about *les Juifs*?" he demanded.

Hugo swept out his arm, as if to take in all the Jewish boys. "The priest says you killed Our Lord Jesus Christ!"

"Killed Christ—us Jews?" Yossi said, not sure he understood.

Hugo nodded.

"That's a lie!"

Hugo's face turned red but he pressed on. "And they say that you Jews kill Christian children to get blood for your rituals."

Yossi couldn't follow that French. "What? What's he saying?"

Together, René and Jean-Paul acted out a gruesome drama of slit throats, cupped hands, gurgling and frenzied prayers.

Yossi's jaw dropped. "That's crazy!"

"Disgusting!" Milton added.

"Besides," Louie put in, "it wouldn't be kosher!"

Hugo looked sheepish. "Well, that's what they say," he mumbled.

René stepped in front of him. "Listen, Hugo, these fellows are all right. They're not the bad ones. Maybe those other ones"—he pointed toward Steiner's—"but not these ones. You got that?"

There was a moment of silence. "Yeah," Hugo said. He glanced at the Jewish boys, and while he wasn't smiling, Yossi saw that he looked a little less hostile.

Yossi tried to think of a way to show that he and his pals had no hard feelings. He whispered to his friends and they nodded eagerly. Leading the French boys to Moishe's pushcart, the Jewish boys pooled their pennies and treated their new friends to pickled herring.

Then the French boys made dessert—by stirring maple syrup into snow! *La crème glacée à l'érable*, they called it, but when it was Yossi's turn to take a bite, he looked at the mixture doubtfully. Whoever heard of eating tree sap mixed into snow? Hesitantly, he put a spoonful in his mouth. Cold! Sweet! Icy! Syrupy! *"Dé- dé- délicieuse!"* he said in his new-found French.

All the boys laughed.

"Now what?" René said.

"Well," Yossi said, "we can't skate. So let's play at something we can all do. How about"—he quickly packed a snow-ball and lobbed it at René—"a snowball fight?"

*"La guerre!"* René shouted, and the air

was soon full of flying snowballs, all the boys running and falling, sliding and laughing, hitting and getting hit.

Even Hugo.

# Chapter Nine

One day, approaching the ice rink with a bundle on his back, Yossi heard yells and howls. He stopped short. There was a crowd of boys on the ice, pushing and poking, kicking and punching, slugging and swinging and shoving.

Yossi ran closer. Where were his friends? There! He made out René...Jacques... Hugo... They were surrounded by nine or ten bigger, stronger boys—and they were getting beaten up!

Yossi dropped his bundle and ran onto the ice. A tall muscular boy had his fist upraised, about to punch Jean-Paul. Yossi grabbed the boy's arm and spun

91

him around. Surprised, the boy lost his balance and fell.

"*Merci!*" Jean-Paul yelled.

"What's going on?" Yossi said.

"*Ils nous ont volé notre glace!*" Jean-Paul said, then went flying as the big boy, back on his feet, hit him with his shoulder.

"Stole your ice!" Yossi repeated. "Oof!" He landed on his bottom, hard, as the same boy gave him a mighty shove.

"Take that, you!" the big boy said in Yiddish.

Yiddish! These boys were Jewish? Yossi scrambled to his feet—and recognized Max Steiner's cronies who'd laughed at him that day outside the synagogue.

Yossi started searching for Max in the crush of bodies, sure that the boss's son was behind this. Yes! There he was, in his once-again-spotless black coat. Sliding across the ice, windmilling his arms, Yossi threw himself against Max.

"You rat!" he yelled in Yiddish. "What do you think you're doing?"

Max whirled around on his skates. There

was a moment of astonishment. Then he leered. "You!" He pushed Yossi down.

Yossi sprang back up. "Thief! You can't take their ice!" He swung at Max.

Max laughed, skating out of the way. "Oh, yeah? We just did. It's ours now."

"Well, you're going to have to get past me!" Yossi shouted as he charged. But Max darted aside, and with a few swift steps he plowed into Yossi, knocking him down again.

Yossi climbed to his feet and kept fighting. But even though he swung wildly, he took a flurry of punches and knew that he was getting the worst of it. What's more, he knew that his friends were too. In a quick scan of the ice, Yossi saw Jacques get socked in the stomach, while René, his nose bleeding and his cheek scratched, sprawled face-down as a boy the size of a man pushed him from behind.

Amid the yelling and grunting, Yossi heard a shrill whistle that he recognized as René's. *On s'en va, les gars!*

Yossi joined the French boys at the edge of the ice, expecting René to rally the boys to drive the intruders away. But instead René picked up his skates and stick. *"Allons-y, les gars. On s'en va."*

"What do you mean, let's go?" Yossi said, grabbing his sleeve. "Aren't you going to chase them away? This is your ice!"

"What do you think we've been trying to do?" René said angrily. "You saw how it was. They're too much for us."

"But you can't just let them—"

"We can't beat them. There's too many and they're too big and strong."

"Then I'll get my pals!" Yossi cried. But even as he said it, he knew it was no use. Even with Abie and Benny and Louie and Milton, they wouldn't be able to fight off these older stronger boys.

Fuming, Yossi stood there with the others and watched as Max and his friends skated triumphantly around the rink, hooting and crowing, slapping each other on the back.

René and the others started walking

away, but Yossi waited for Max to skate by. "You're nothing but a dirty rotten *gonef*, Steiner."

Max's face darkened. "Who are you calling a thief, you stinking *griner*? You peasant!" He drew closer. "I know it was you who threw the eggs, and I know your Frenchie pals hid you that day. You think you're so smart. Well, how smart do you feel right now, huh?"

"Smart enough to get you back for this!"

"Oh, yeah? You, the big strong *shlepper* of bundles?" With a laugh, Max skated away.

Yossi grabbed his bundle and caught up with René and the boys. "Now what?"

"Now we find another spot," René answered, "and build a rink from scratch."

The boys wandered up one street and down another, searching for a good spot. One alley with a promising dip in the middle had too much horse and wagon traffic. There was a ditch in an out-of-the-way lane, but it was too narrow. Finally they came to an alley behind a row of little-used shops. There was a mound of lumber scraps and garbage in the middle, and the alley was narrower at one end than the other. But it sloped down at the center, and it was so pocked with potholes that it didn't look as if anyone traveled that way. At the corner was a hand pump with a long metal arm.

René grunted. "Here. Tomorrow morning. Bring pails and shovels and wheelbarrows, boys."

The next day, Yossi showed up with Abie, Benny, Louie and Milton. Together, the boys carted away armfuls and barrow-loads of scraps, garbage, rocks and debris. They filled buckets of water at the pump and emptied them into the trench. Slowly the water level rose.

At first they grumbled as they worked. "*Sales Anglais*...Rotten thieves..." Then the French boys began to sing. "*Alouette, gentille alouette...*" in rhythm with the

passing of the buckets. They taught the Jewish boys their song, and the Jewish boys taught them "My Rumania, My Rumania." Neither group understood the words of the other's song, but they parrotted the sounds and laughed at one another's mistakes.

The boys waited overnight for the water to freeze, then came back the next day, and the day after that, and did it again. Finally, after four days, the ice was level with the ground.

The assembled boys stood and regarded their new rink. It was bumpy in places, gouged in others. It sloped toward the low side of the alley. It was wide at one end, narrow at the other.

"Beautiful, *non*?" Michel said.

"Yeah," the others chorused.

Yossi didn't chime in. As far as he was concerned, the new rink wasn't nearly as good as the one they'd lost. And he knew that Max Steiner must have been behind it. He must have seen the rink the day he and the supervisor had chased Yossi and decided then and there to take it away from the French boys.

Well, he'd done it.

But as Yossi's friends slid happily on the new sheet of ice, the French boys on skates holding up the Jewish boys in boots, he made a silent vow. Somehow he'd pay Max Steiner back.

# Chapter Ten

Something was up. Something was definitely up. Daniel and Miriam were going out more frequently than ever, looking over their shoulders as they came and went. Yossi heard new phrases: "protest march…labor action…ultimatum."

One night Solly came over, accompanied by Abie's father, Herman, and Josef, a stitcher who operated a machine a few rows over from Papa. The five of them—Daniel, Miriam, Solly, Herman and Josef—huddled around the kitchen table. Papa greeted everyone, then went into the bedroom, pointedly not joining in. As they started talking, Papa loudly rustled the pages of *Die Zeit* as if he were devouring every word. Even so, Yossi noticed that the rustling grew less and less frequent as the conversation—which was all about timing and whistles and doors—went on. Yossi couldn't imagine what it was all about.

Later, after the visitors left, Papa came out, arms folded across his chest, a worried look on his face. "Now what crazy plan are you hatching?"

Miriam and Daniel exchanged a look. "A walkout, Papa," Miriam said.

"What!" Papa shouted. "Are you mad?"

"Papa, shaaah!" Miriam hissed. "The neighbors'll hear."

"What's a walkout?" Yossi asked.

"It's a disaster, that's what," Papa said. "An invitation to get arrested—"

Ignoring him, Daniel turned to Yossi. "It means that the workers are going to walk out of the sweatshop—"

"To protest their working conditions—," Miriam added.

"And not go back until Steiner agrees to improve things."

"And not just at Steiner's, at the other two sweatshops too."

"Walk out how?" Yossi asked.

Daniel grinned. "Picture this, Yossi. It'll be just like a normal day. Everybody'll go to work, just like usual."

"Even me?" Yossi said.

"Even you," Miriam said. "Everybody. The cutters, the carriers, the stitchers. Just like a normal day. So nobody'll suspect anything."

Daniel continued, "The men'll start up their machines, just like usual. Start sewing, cutting, whatever. At a certain time, I'll give a signal and turn off my sewing machine. The same with Solly, Herman and Josef, in different areas of the factory. And then the men around us will do the same. Shut off their machines, put down their scissors, lay down their tape measures. We'll get up and walk out. And the same thing will happen at the other sweatshops."

Yossi gasped, imagining hundreds of men marching out of the building.

Papa groaned.

"And the women will meet them there," Miriam said excitedly. "We'll have a big protest right in front of Steiner's."

"How exciting!" Yossi began, but Papa clapped his hands to his head. "Not only my crazy son-in-law, but my daughter too will get her head bashed in."

"Don't be silly, Papa," Miriam said.

"And besides, it'll never work," Papa went on anxiously. "The men are too scared to walk out. And if—"

"Not anymore, Papa," Miriam said. "They're fed up. Sickness, low pay, long hours, failing eyesight. It's the same at all the sweatshops, and the workers aren't going to take it anymore. They're ready."

Daniel nodded. "When one walks out, another will follow. And another and another. When the workers see that their fellows are with them, everyone will join in, Avram. You'll see."

"Not with Steiner's goons on hand, ready to club back anyone who dares to leave his machine!" Papa said in an agonized voice. "And then what? They see one of their fellows get beaten up, they'll back out. The whole thing'll be a failure. And Steiner'll find out who the leaders were, and then—"

"That's why Steiner can't know!" Daniel interrupted. "So he's taken by surprise and doesn't have a chance to call in his goons ahead of time. That's the only way it can work."

Miriam turned to Yossi. "Daniel's right, Yossele. It has to be a secret. Even the workers don't know exactly when it'll be, only the leaders. So you can't tell anyone."

"Not even Abie?" Yossi said. "After all, his papa is in on it—"

"Not even Abie," Daniel said. "We can't risk having you talk to him about it, in case someone overhears and it gets back to Steiner. We shouldn't even have told you."

"You can trust me! My lips are sealed!"

Miriam tousled Yossi's hair. "We know, Yossele. You're a good comrade."

Yossi grinned. Then he quickly clamped his lips shut.

The next morning, Yossi ran into Abie at *Die Zeit*. He threw his arm around his friend. "Hi, Abie, old pal!"

Abie gave him a look. "What's up with you?"

"Oh, nothing. Just saying hi to my *comrade*."

A light went on in Abie's eyes. Yossi wriggled, he was so frustrated by not being able to talk over the exciting news with his friend.

Abie received his stack of papers and started for the door.

"Wait for me," Yossi said. "We'll *walk out* together."

Abie giggled. "Okay." Once outside, he leaned close. "Can't say anything to anybody."

Yossi made a slash across his throat as if to show that he'd sooner die than tell Daniel's secret.

A few nights later, Solly, Herman and Josef came over again. This time, they pored over a large sheet of paper that was spread out on the table. Yossi peeked around Daniel's arm. There was a big rectangle drawn on the paper, with lines and arrows marked on it. The men and Miriam were discussing "stairways" and "exits" and "marshalling areas."

Huh? Yossi wondered. What were they talking about? And what did those lines on the paper have to do with stairways?

"That's not a good plan," Yossi heard a new voice say. He looked up. Papa! Papa was at the table!

"Avram," Herman said, clapping him on the back, "you're joining us?"

Papa colored slightly. "I still think it's a crazy scheme. I wouldn't even dream of getting involved, but...well, I feel it's my duty to help this hothead here stay out of jail, so he should be around to take care of my daughter."

Yossi saw that although Papa was trying not to appear too interested, he kept sneaking looks at the paper on the table. Yossi hid a smile.

"A father's got to do his duty," Josef said solemnly. "So, Avram, why isn't it a good plan?"

"Because Morris—you know, the fat supervisor with the loud voice—is always standing by the front door." Papa pointed to a thick line in the middle of the bottom side of the rectangle.

Following Papa's finger, Yossi realized that what he was looking at was a map of Steiner's Garment Works. Now the marks made sense. He made out the staircase that led up to Steiner's office from the hallway near the packing room, and the broad steps leading up to the double front doors.

Daniel shot Papa a grateful look. "You're right, Avram. I hadn't thought of that."

Papa pointed to another set of marks. "It makes more sense to have the men walk out through the side doors. They're near the exits to the privies. So if people start heading in that direction, it won't look suspicious."

"Not for a while, anyway," Josef said, "until the supervisors realize there's an awful lot of men heeding the call of nature."

Yossi giggled.

"Avram's right," Herman said. "We can move workers faster out of both sides of the building, and then they can move around to the front."

"Once things get underway, once the men are moving in numbers and it's too late to stop them, then we can use the front door, and even the back loading dock," Papa added.

*We*, Yossi thought. He said *we*.

"An excellent idea, Avram," Daniel said. He winked at Yossi. Yossi grinned back. So Papa was turning into a labor agitator too!

# Chapter Eleven

*Come on, somebody! Come buy my last paper!* Yossi thought, wriggling with excitement. That morning, Daniel had pulled him aside and told him that today was the day. Yossi and Abie had arranged that, as soon as they sold their papers, Abie would get Louie, Benny and Milton, and Yossi would round up René and the French boys. They'd bring all of them to Steiner's to see the fun.

Yossi had sold his first eleven newspapers in minutes, but it was taking forever to get rid of the last one. Finally, an old man came by pushing a barrow of stacked wood.

"More pogroms in Russia! New boatloads to arrive in Montreal! Read all about it!" Yossi yelled in Yiddish.

The man took the paper. *Finally!* Yossi thought. He was about to run off, but the man grabbed him by the sleeve. "Please, boy, read to me about the pogroms. I've got to know if my family's safe."

Yossi was longing to go, but he took one look at the man's face and started riffling through the pages. "Fires, beatings, executions...Smolensk...Rudnya... Yartsevo..."

"What about Novgorod?" The old man pressed close.

Yossi scanned the page. "Nothing about Novgorod."

"Thank God." The man wiped his eyes. "Thank you, lad. God bless you."

"That's all right. Bye!" Yossi took off. Just his luck if he was too late for all the excitement, he thought, as he ran to the new rink to round up René and the gang. Waving his arms, he yelled in his new-found French, *"Venez vite! Venez vite!"*

110

René peered down the street. "They after you again?"

"No, no, nothing like that. But something is going to happen. Something big. You've got to come with me."

"Come with you where?" Hugo asked.

"To Steiner's." Some of the boys hesitated, but to Yossi's surprise, Hugo said, "Listen, boys, if Yossi says come, we'd better come."

Yossi flashed him a smile, and the boys changed from skates to boots. Yossi hurried them along, brushing off their questions with a smile and a shake of the head. When Steiner's came into sight, no one was gathered out front. There was no sign yet of Abie and the boys.

He stopped under a maple tree across the street from the factory. "Okay, boys, wait here. I've got to go pick up my bundle. Be right back."

"I'm coming with you," René said.

"You can't go in there!"

"I want to see what it's like."

"But what if they see you?"

René smiled. "I'll be like a ghost."

Leaving the others behind, the two boys entered at the side door near the packing room. Yossi pointed to a shadowy alcove beside the door. "Wait there," he whispered, "and if anyone comes, leave—fast!"

René nodded and Yossi went into the packing room. Solly winked at him, then quickly looked away as the supervisor stormed over. "You're late!" he snapped. "I should dock you a day's pay—" Yossi started to answer, but the supervisor went on, "And you too!"

Yossi looked over his shoulder. Abie! Yossi hadn't heard him come in.

"Sorry, sir," Yossi said. "We'll be quick."

"You'd better be, or else you're through here. Is that clear?" the supervisor said.

"Yes, sir," Yossi and Abie said together.

The two of them got their bundles and went back into the hallway. "Whew," Yossi whispered. Then his eye was caught by René's frantic hand motions. He was pointing down the hallway.

Yossi and Abie turned. Midway down

the hall was a small storage room where Steiner kept scraps and odd pieces of fabric. Farther down the hall was a door to a stairway that led up to Steiner's office. At the end of the hall was a door to the sweatshop floor.

Voices could be heard from the end of the hallway. But the door to the scrap room was open, and it was blocking the speakers from view.

Yossi exchanged a panic-stricken look with Abie and René. Then he motioned them to follow. The three boys tiptoed down the hall and hid behind the open scrap room door, Yossi and Abie silently shrugging off their bundles. Yossi felt a tug on his sleeve. René was pointing again. On the floor was a pair of hockey skates—brand-new hockey skates—and a smart black winter coat with brass buttons.

Max Steiner!

*What's he doing here?* Yossi wondered.

"Listen, they're planning a big protest today," a voice said in Yiddish. It was older...high-pitched...familiar... "Don't know exactly when, but someone is going to give a signal."

"Who, Jonah?" Max said.

*Jonah Fishkin!* Yossi thought. That dirty rat!

"I don't know," Jonah grumbled. "Couldn't get the inside information this time."

With a pang of guilt, Yossi remembered that he had meant to warn Daniel about Jonah, and had forgotten—again. At least Jonah didn't know who was behind the plan.

"But it's going to be big," Jonah went on. "Something about refusing to work—"

"What! We've got to stop them!" Max cried. "Sound the alarm!"

"No, no," Jonah said, "that'll tip them off that we know. Better to warn your papa on the quiet. That way he can get men in place before they start. That'll stop them, all right."

"Yes, that's it!" Max said. "I'll go tell Papa right now."

"Don't forget to tell him who told you," Jonah added slyly.

*You weasel!* Yossi thought, exchanging an angry glance with Abie.

"I won't. Good work, Fishkin," Max said.

"I'd better get back before I'm missed," Jonah said. "See you later."

A door opened, and for a moment the hallway was filled with the roar and screech of the factory floor. Then it clicked shut and the noise subsided to a muffled hum. Yossi thought frantically. They had to stop Max Steiner from getting word to his father. But how? If they grabbed Max, he'd start screaming, and that would alert everybody.

Yossi heard footsteps. Max was heading for the door that led up to his papa's office. They had to do something—now. Yossi glanced about, desperate for an idea, and again saw the skates and coat.

Yes!

Still hidden behind the scrap room door he said loudly in Yiddish, "Oh, look, somebody left a pair of hockey skates. Guess he didn't want them anymore. I sure could use a new pair—"

"What's that? Who's there?" Max's voice said, sounding startled.

Yossi was ready. As Max flung back the scrap room door to see who was on the other side, Yossi grabbed Max's fancy winter coat, flung it over Max's head and wrapped it around him, pinning his arms to the sides. René held the hood against Max's thrashing head, while Abie and Yossi kept Max's arms pinned to his body. Max tried to yell, but his cries were muffled by the thick wool, and even though he twisted and kicked, Yossi and Abie were able to keep him from getting away.

They hustled their prisoner into the scrap room and threw him face down onto soft piles of felt and gabardine, muslin and cotton. Yossi could feel Max's fear in his desperate thrashing. Despite himself, he felt sorry for the other boy. He would have been scared too, if he'd been grabbed like that. He knelt close. "Don't worry," he whispered, "we're not going to hurt you."

Max's squirming grew less frantic, but he was still twisting about, clearly trying to escape. Yossi tied his feet together with a length of burlap, doubling the thickness so it wouldn't hurt, and Abie did the same with his hands. Yossi grabbed several pieces of felt for a gag. Soft and fuzzy, they'd be just the thing to muffle any noise that Max might make.

The boys rolled him over and Yossi slapped the felt pieces against his mouth.

"You'll never get away with this!" Max managed to get out. "Just wait until my papa—"

"But your papa's not going to know," Yossi said, pushing the fabric against Max's lips and motioning Abie to tie a sturdy length of cotton around his head to hold them in place. "Because you're not going to tell him. Because you're going to stay here, nice and quiet."

Max made a muffled noise that Yossi was sure wasn't at all polite.

"We just need you out of the way for a while," Yossi told him. "We'll let you out soon, I promise."

Max glared at him, but Yossi saw that there was relief in his eyes, as well as anger.

Yossi motioned to René and Abie. The three of them crept to the door and peeked out. The two bundles were where the boys had left them. There was no one in the hallway. Saying a silent prayer of thanks, Yossi waved his arm forward. He and Abie helped each other on with their bundles, and the three boys tiptoed down the hallway and out the door.

Fresh air! Freedom! Safety!

Yossi hurried across the street, followed by Abie and René. Benny, Louie and Milton had joined the French boys under the maple tree, and now they all rushed forward.

"Where were you?"

"*Qu'est-ce qui a pris si longtemps?*"

"What's going on?"

Yossi grinned. "We're fine! It was a close call, but everything's going to be all right."

"Everything *what?*" Benny asked in an agonized voice.

Yossi and Abie laughed. "You'll see—soon. Come around here and watch."

They led the others to the foot of the broad steps at the front of the factory—and they didn't have long to wait. After several minutes, a piercing whistle shrieked over the din of the sewing machines. Yossi caught Abie's eye. "The signal!" he said.

Another whistle. Another. A minute passed. Nothing happened. Then, gradually, the factory's noise began to change. It grew a little quieter, such a small change that Yossi wasn't sure if he really heard it. Then quieter still. Slowly the roar changed to a drone, the drone to a hum.

Men began to appear at the sides of the sweatshop. At first one or two, then half a dozen, then a steady trickle. In pairs and groups, they came down the stairs at either side of the building and marched around to the front, where they gathered at the base of the staircase, in front of the boys.

"They're...walking out!" Benny said in amazement.

"*Mon dieu!*" Jean-Paul said.

Yossi and Abie just grinned at the others.

The din of the machines grew even softer and quieter. Still, the men poured out the side doors and others began to come around from the back. The noise of the factory faded, faded. The massive double front doors swung open, and men began to pour down the front steps. Supervisors appeared at the top of the stairs, pointing back toward the factory and yelling, but the workers ignored them, continuing to file outside in an unbroken stream.

With a final whir, the machines fell silent. A cheer arose from the men gathered outside. They slapped one another on the back.

Craning for a better view, Yossi spotted a familiar tweed cap at the top of the stairs. "Daniel!" he shouted, waving his cap. Daniel turned, flashed Yossi a grin and waved his cap. Then Yossi saw Papa waving. "We did it, Papa!" he yelled, and even though he couldn't hear Papa's reply, he laughed as Papa waved his cap back.

"There's *my* papa!" Abie said. "Papa!" he hollered, and Herman turned and pumped his fist in the air.

"Papa!" Jean-Paul shouted, and a short man waved back, grinning.

"Look!" Milton cried, and Yossi turned. Women and girls of all ages were coming down the side streets leading to the factory. When the men saw them, a shout went up, a deep rumble that was answered by a high female cheer. Yossi saw Miriam, Mama and Sadie, and he waved madly. Miriam waved back, and then Yossi lost sight of her as she pushed into the crowd. A few moments later, her blue-kerchiefed head appeared beside Daniel's shoulder.

There was a commotion at the top of the stairs, and a heavyset man in a long black topcoat and fur hat emerged. Mr.

Steiner! Even from this distance, Yossi could see that his face was red. He waved his arms, gesturing toward the factory, but the workers ignored him. He lifted a bullhorn to his mouth and bellowed, "You men, get back to work!"

No one paid attention.

"You think you can just walk out on the job? Well, you can't."

"We just did, boss," someone yelled, and there was a chorus of laughter.

"I'm warning you, get back to your machines right away!"

"We're not going, Steiner," Daniel shouted, stepping forward.

Mr. Steiner pointed at him. "You! Bernstein! I should have known you'd be the ringleader."

Yossi swelled with pride. His almost-brother-in-law, the ringleader! But then a thought struck him. If Mr. Steiner knew that Daniel was behind this, he might fire him. And Papa and Solly and Herman and Josef too. Then what would happen?

The next moment, one of the garment packers yelled, "He's not the ringleader, Steiner. I am!"

"No!" Another man waved his arm in the air. "I am!"

"No! It was me!"

"I'm the ringleader!"

"I started it!"

One after another, dozens of men—and women too—hollered out that they were responsible for the walkout. Mr. Steiner turned to look at first one, then another, his face growing redder and redder.

"It was all of us!" Solly yelled. A great shout went up. As if on signal, hundreds of men and women linked arms with the people on either side of them.

"You're going to have to fire us all, Steiner!" yelled Herman, and cries of agreement rang out.

"Then that's just what I'll do!" Mr. Steiner bellowed. "There are plenty of others to take your place—"

"I wouldn't count on it, Steiner," Josef shouted. "Our comrades walked out of two other sweatshops today. No one's going to put up with these conditions anymore!"

A look of shock came over Mr. Steiner's face.

"That's right, Mr. Steiner," Daniel shouted. "No more starvation wages."

A cheer.

"No more dust and damp that make us sick," yelled another man.

A shout.

"No more working from dawn to dusk with hardly a break," added another.

A holler. "And we're not coming back to work for you until you agree," Miriam shouted.

Her hand, clasped in Daniel's, shot into the air, and a roar went up from the workers that was even louder than the factory at full production.

Mr. Steiner stood there, staring at the crowd. He raised the bullhorn to his lips, then lowered it. His face grew redder. He turned on his heel and stomped inside, followed by his thugs.

Hundreds of caps flew into the air, and the cheer that rose out of hundreds of throats seemed to shake the very bricks of Steiner's Garment Works.

Yossi cheered along with his friends. Then he hurried around to the side entrance and snuck into the scrap room. Max Steiner was sitting up. When Yossi came in, his head whipped around. For a moment there was fear in his eyes. Then he glared.

Yossi untied the gag.

"You—you dog!" Max snapped, twisting from side to side.

"Hold still! I'm trying to untie you," Yossi said. He couldn't blame Max for being angry, but the least he could do was let Yossi free him!

Max kept still long enough for Yossi to loosen the burlap around his hands, then untied his own feet. He jumped up with a sneer. "Just wait till I tell my papa what you did. He'll fire you—you and your whole family! And your stupid friend too. All of you. You'll never work here again!"

Yossi smiled. "That's what you think. All the workers walked out of all the sweatshops in the neighborhood today. It's not going to be so easy to replace them."

Max's hand flew to his mouth. "All the workers...? They can't!"

Yossi stepped forward, eyes blazing. "Yes, they can—and they did! Your papa is going to have to treat us better from now on—like decent human beings." He strode to the door. "I'm sorry I tied you up. I had to. But I'm not sorry I helped, no matter what happens to me. Not one bit!"

The door slammed behind him as he ran down the hall.

# Chapter Twelve

Yossi carried an armful of books down the three flights of stairs and dumped them in a wheelbarrow sitting outside the front door. On his way back upstairs, he passed Daniel coming down carrying a box of dishes, followed by Miriam with an armload of clothing. Yossi made another trip with more books, filling the wheelbarrow to overflowing.

When he went back upstairs, Miriam was pulling on her tattered shawl.

"You don't need to go with him, Miriam," Mama scolded. "Daniel can push the wheelbarrow four blocks by himself. Better stay and do more packing."

Miriam linked her arm through Daniel's. "But Mama, I want to go with my *husband*."

Everybody laughed, and Sadie sighed. "Such lovebirds. Ah, let them go, Gussie. We'll pack."

Mama shook her head. "Five minutes she can't be away from him." But she was smiling.

Yossi smiled too. Although Mr. Steiner had suspected that Daniel really was the ringleader and wanted to fire him, he hadn't been able to prove it. His spy, Jonah Fishkin, couldn't identify the leaders. When Mr. Steiner had threatened to fire Daniel anyway, all the workers threatened to walk out again. And the workers at all three sweatshops vowed to stay out until the owners raised their wages and improved their working conditions.

The factories stayed closed for a week. Yossi began to worry, and even though Daniel and Miriam were acting brave, Yossi knew they were worried. But Mr.

Steiner and the other owners must have been losing too much money—or finally realized that they weren't going to be able to treat the workers as they had—because they reluctantly agreed to some of the demands: to raise wages, put in fans and shorten the work day by a quarter of an hour.

The raise wasn't much—barely a pittance—but for Miriam and Daniel, it was enough. They'd immediately gotten married and found a tiny flat in a broken-down tenement building a few blocks away.

Now, Daniel pulled on his cap. Turning to Miriam and crooking his arm, he said, "Shall we, my dear wife?"

She linked her arm through his. "Yes, my darling husband."

They kissed noisily.

"Yuch!" Yossi said. Then he brightened. "At least you can do that at your own place now. I don't have to watch!"

Everybody laughed.

At last, the moment had come. Yossi sat on a hard-packed snowbank and tugged on his new ice skates.

Just a week or so ago, he'd thought his dream of owning skates was gone forever. Mr. Steiner might not have been able to figure out who to blame for the walkout, but he knew exactly who to blame for tying up his son. Yossi and Abie had been fired and told never to show their faces at Steiner's Garment Works again.

Yossi knew that Abie's family desperately needed what Abie earned. And Yossi was worried about his skates. Without the income from hauling bundles, how would he ever save enough?

But when word got around about what the boys had done for the walkout, the publisher of *Die Zeit* had offered them work delivering stacks of newspapers to different shops in the neighborhood—at better wages than they'd earned hauling garments.

Even with the extra money, Yossi still didn't have enough to buy a brand-new pair of skates. But René had taken him to a secondhand store in the French section. After a rapid explanation by René, accompanied by many heart-rending facial expressions cast in Yossi's direction, the shopkeeper had brought out a pair of skates from the back room. The toes were worn through, the blades were tarnished and one tongue was cracked and split. They were in the back because nobody wanted them.

"They're the most beautiful skates I've ever seen," Yossi breathed.

Now, he laced them up, wrapping the laces around his ankles like he'd seen the other boys do. He grabbed a stick that Jean-Paul had loaned him and pushed himself to his feet. And promptly fell on his bottom.Carefully leaning on the stick, he stood up.

This time he fell on his face.

Spitting out ice shavings, he pushed himself to his knees. "This is harder than I thought," he said.

One foot up. Stick in position. Lean… push off…other foot…up! He was standing. He took a choppy step. Still upright! Another step—and he went sprawling again. Laughing, René and Jean-Paul skated over. Each taking an arm, they lifted Yossi to his feet. "Here you go," René said. "Left, right, left, right…" This was more like it—he was actually skating!

Until they let go.

On all fours, Yossi watched Hugo drop the lump of coal, and the game began. Today, Michel's younger brother Pierre had come. Pierre and Michel were each tending goal at opposite ends of the ice, allowing two teams of three—Jean-Paul, Georges and Jacques against René, Hugo and Yossi—to battle each other.

Yossi struggled to his feet in time to see Jean-Paul whiz by, followed by René. Yossi took a couple of wobbly steps after them. René knocked Jean-Paul's stick off the lump of coal, spun around and passed it down the ice to Hugo. The play quickly moved in the opposite direction.

Yossi swung around to follow them and immediately fell on his face.

"*Ici!*" René yelled, tapping his stick. But as Hugo passed the lump of coal, Jacques intercepted and, with a shout of "Georges!" sent it spinning toward his brother.

Yossi pushed himself up and headed toward Georges, leaning on his stick. One step...two steps...three...

"*Ici, Georges!*" Georges passed to Jean-Paul, and the lump of coal tumbled in Yossi's direction. He reached out his stick—and went sprawling, stopping only when he smashed into the snowbank at the side of the ice.

"Oof!" he said, coming up with a face full of snow. On his knees, he watched as Jean-Paul shot on goal, but Pierre batted the lump away.

"Hah!"

"*Zut!*"

René skated over and got control of the lump of coal. With a scrape of blades, Jacques moved in and tried to bump

René's stick off the coal, but René sent it spinning toward Hugo, who took three quick strides to grab it before Georges could intercept.

Knees aching, elbows sore, Yossi pushed himself up. Stick down, foot forward. One step, another...Hugo passed the lump back across the ice to René, who started skating toward goal. Wobbling, but staying upright, Yossi followed. Georges charged René, but René zigzagged sideways to keep the lump out of reach. Yossi chugged on, one step, two, three... Now he was even with René...now he was past René...now he was closing in on the goal.

Speedy Jean-Paul darted up behind René, bumping his stick, but René held on. He looked up.

"René! Here!" Yossi yelled.

René passed. As Yossi took another step, reaching forward with his stick, Jean-Paul bumped him, sending him flying. "Oooof!" Yossi yelled, starting to fall. Wildly careening on one blade, tilting sideways, he flailed with his stick. The tip

of his stick nicked the coal. The lump rose off the ice. Michel moved his stick.

Yossi crashed onto the ice as the lump of coal soared. His stick, swooping downward, tripped Rene, who sprawled beside him.

Michel's goal stick rose. Too late! As the goaltender started to topple over, felled by Yossi's stick, the lump of coal flew past him and lodged in the snowbank.

"Goal!" Yossi shouted in amazement. Face full of ice, sliding into the goal crease in a tangle of sticks and skates and arms and legs, he laughed out loud. "Goal!"

# Author's Note

Starting in the early 1880s, tens of thousands of Jews fled pogroms, or massacres, in Eastern Europe and Russia, and emigrated to the United States and Canada. Although these immigrants were grateful to live in countries that allowed religious freedom, their lives were hard. They lived in cramped, unsanitary apartment buildings called tenements. For many, the only work they could get was in garment factories—called sweatshops—where they worked ten to fifteen hours a day in noisy, crowded, poorly lit rooms for as little as $1 to $2 per week. Young children lugged bundles of cut-out garment pieces to tenements where girls and women sewed them, and then lugged the finished garments back.

Because of the appalling conditions in the sweatshops, workers began to protest. They tried to form labor unions in order to stand together against the owners. They held walkouts and strikes.

For many years, these protests were unsuccessful. The owners simply fired any workers who refused to work, or called in the police to arrest them. Although *Yossi's Goal* suggests that the owners agreed to improve working conditions as early as the 1890s, the unions did not make any real progress until about 1915. Gradually, however, the protests began to have an effect, and the garment workers won the right to a reasonable work week, healthier working conditions and a decent wage.

# Glossary

| | |
|---|---|
| Babushka | Headscarf |
| Bima | Raised platform at the front of a synagogue |
| Cossacks | Soldiers serving the Russian czars |
| *Die Zeit* | *The Times*; a Yiddish newspaper in Montreal |
| Gonef | Thief |
| Griner | Recent immigrant who is poor and uneducated |
| Kosher | Food prepared according to Jewish dietary laws |
| Landsmanschaft | Organization set up to aid countrymen |
| Pogrom | An organized massacre of helpless people |
| Rebbe | Rabbi |
| Rosh Hashanah | Jewish New Year |
| Schul | Synagogue or temple |
| Shabbas | Sabbath |
| Shabbat Shalom | Good Sabbath |
| Shlep | Carry |
| Shmata | Rag |

| | |
|---|---|
| Torah | Holy scrolls |
| Tzedakeh | Social justice; the duty of those with more to help those with less. (In Judaism, there is no word for charity.) |
| Yarmelke | Men's head covering |
| Yuntov | Happy holiday |

**Ellen Schwartz**'s grandparents emigrated to North America at about the same time, and in similar circumstances, as Yossi's family. In order to learn about early Jewish immigrant life, she did lots of research in Montreal, a city that she loves. Ellen is the author of many books for children, including the Starshine series, *I Love Yoga!* and *Jesse's Star* (Orca), the first book about the irrepressible Yossi. She lives in Burnaby, British Columbia.